WHAT MAKES A FLOWER GROW?

Susan Mayes

Designed by Mike Pringle
Illustrated by Brin Edwards and Mike Pringle

Revised by Philippa Wingate
Cover design by Russell Punter
Cover illustration by Christyan Fox
With thanks to Katarina Dragoslavić and Rosie Dickins

Series editor: Heather Amery

CONTENTS

All about flowers

Thousands of different flowers grow all over the world. They grow in gardens, on vegetables, on trees, in streets, in hedges and in your home.

Flowers are all kinds of colours, shapes and sizes. Some of them have very strong smells.

Insects and other tiny animals visit them. Most flowers die each year and grow again later.

2

Some flowers live in very hot countries and others live in cold places. Very strange flowers grow in some parts of the world.

Why do flowers have different colours and smells? Why do they grow again and what do they need to grow well?

What are the strangest flowers? You can find out about all of these things in this book.

Taking a close look

If you look closely at a flower, you can see that it has different parts. Each part has a special job.

Looking at a poppy

A baby flower, called a bud, grows safely inside two sepals.

Sepal

Bud

Sepals protect the bud and stop birds and insects from eating it.

Petal

As the bud grows, it opens up and the petals stretch out.

The stigma is sticky. It grows on top of the pistil.

The pistil is in the middle of the flower. New seeds will grow inside. It is sometimes called the seed box.

Pistil

Stigma

Stamen

The stamens grow around the pistil.

On top of each stamen there are tiny specks of golden dust, called pollen.

---

4 **Internet link** Go to **www.usborne-quicklinks.com** and enter the keywords "pocket flower" for a link to a Web site where you can print out and label a flower diagram.

Different flowers

Most flowers have the same main parts, but they are all kinds of different colours, shapes and sizes.

A yellow water lily has big sepals around the outside and lots of short petals in the middle.

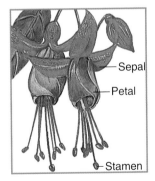

Fuchsias have long stamens and colourful sepals and petals.

A daffodil has one long stigma which grows from the pistil.

The petals of the snapdragon are all joined together.

Who visits a flower?

Flowers all over the world are visited by small animals, birds and many kinds of insects.

Tiny birds

A hummingbird hovers in front of brightly coloured flowers to drink the nectar with its long beak.

Bats

In some countries, bats fly to flowers which open in the evening. They search for nectar and pollen.

Most animals go to flowers to look for pollen and sweet liquid food inside, called nectar.

Honey bees visit all kinds of flowers, looking for food to store for the winter.

Butterflies settle on buddleia flowers to drink nectar with their long tongues.

A bumble bee crawls into a foxglove to find the sweet food.

Flower signals

Many flowers use special signals which make the insects and tiny creatures come to visit them.

Colours

Special colours and markings guide bees to flowers and show them where to find the pollen inside.

You cannot see some markings but bees can. They do not see colours and shapes the same way as we do.

Smells

Most flowers have a sweet smell. It comes from the petals and tells visitors there is food nearby.

Honeysuckle has a strong smell at night. This is when the moths come out to find nectar for food.

A nasty smell

Flies visit a stapelia flower to lay their eggs. They come because it looks and smells like rotting meat.

Internet link Go to www.usborne-quicklinks.com and enter the keywords "pocket flower" for a link to a Web site where you can find out how to train honeybees to visit a cardboard flower.

Visitors at work

Insects and other small animals help plants when visiting them for food.

They carry pollen from flower to flower. This will make seeds grow.

When a bee lands on a flower, some pollen from the stamens rubs off on to its body.

The bee flies to the next flower and some pollen rubs off on to the flower's stigma.

More pollen sticks to the bee as it crawls around on each flower it visits.

Open or closed

Flowers are not open to visitors if the weather is bad. They close to keep the pollen dry and safe.

A day-time flower closes up its petals at night to stop the dew from wetting the pollen inside.

Pollen in the air

Some plants' pollen is carried from plant to plant by the wind.

Tiny grains

Some trees have flowers called catkins. Their tiny, golden grains of pollen blow away in the wind.

Grass has flowers at the top of the stalk. The pollen is high up so it blows away easily.

Pollen clouds

In the summer, you can sometimes see clouds of pollen in the air. People who suffer from hay fever sneeze and sneeze.

Did you know?

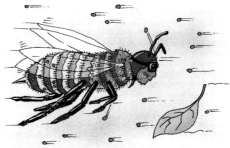

Pollen grains carried by flower visitors are sticky, but pollen grains in the air are smooth and dry.

Internet link Go to *www.usborne-quicklinks.com* and enter the keywords "pocket flower" for a link to a Web site where you can play a matching game and learn more about different parts of a plant.

All about seeds

A plant cannot grow seeds until pollen reaches its stigma. And the pollen must be from the same kind of plant.

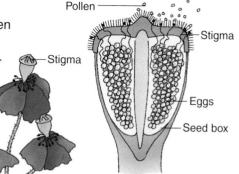

1. Grains of pollen, carried by visitors, or blown by the wind, land on a new flower. They stick to the stigma.

2. The grains travel down into the tiny eggs inside the seed box. They make the eggs grow into seeds.

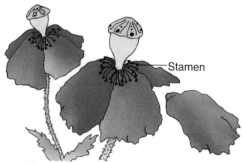

3. The flower doesn't need its petals and stamens any more, so they drop off. Only the seed box is left.

4. The seeds grow inside until they are ripe. The seeds of this plant leave through small holes.

Kinds of seeds

Many different plants have seeds which you can eat.

Sweet chestnuts, walnuts and coconuts are three kinds of seeds which come from trees.

Sunflower seeds are used to make oil and margarine. You can also eat them from the flower.

Inside and outside

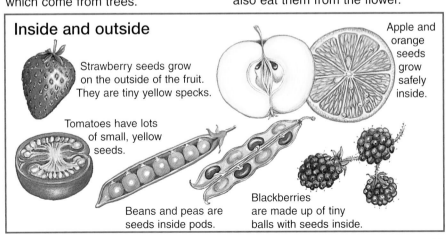

Strawberry seeds grow on the outside of the fruit. They are tiny yellow specks.

Apple and orange seeds grow safely inside.

Tomatoes have lots of small, yellow seeds.

Beans and peas are seeds inside pods.

Blackberries are made up of tiny balls with seeds inside.

Seeds on the move

Popping out

The seeds of an iris grow inside colourful, round fruit. When the fruit is ripe, the seeds leave by popping out on to the ground.

Old Man's Beard

This is the name for the big, fluffy balls from a clematis plant. They are carried by the wind, with the seeds inside.

Seeds leave plants in different ways. Most of them are blown in the wind or are carried by animals.

Birds like to eat brightly coloured seeds. They carry them away.

Seeds with hooks or sticky hairs, stick to birds and animals.

Conkers are the seeds of horse chestnut trees. They fall to the ground in green, spiky cases.

Seeds from a sycamore tree spin to the ground like helicopters.

Dandelion seeds blow away in the wind.

When poppy seeds are ripe, they pop out of the pod.

Ants carry some seeds away and store them for winter food.

Many of the seeds will die or be eaten, but some are covered by soil or leaves. They stay there all winter until spring comes.

Rolling along

Tumbleweeds grow in America. When their seeds are ripe the plant curls into a ball. It rolls along in the wind, scattering the seeds.

The fastest seeds

The Squirting Cucumber plant fills up with water and squirts its seeds out. They travel at about 100 kilometres (60 miles) an hour.

Internet link Go to www.usborne-quicklinks.com and enter the keywords "pocket flower" for a link to a Web site where you can read more about how seeds travel.

Roots and shoots

In the spring, days grow longer and warmer. Seeds get the warmth and rain they need to make them grow.

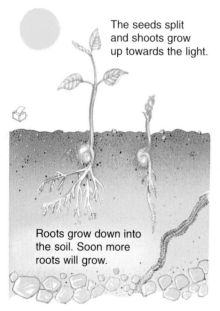

The seeds split and shoots grow up towards the light.

Roots grow down into the soil. Soon more roots will grow.

The roots feed the plant with water and goodness from the soil. They also hold the plant in the ground.

Leaves and sunlight

Little seed leaves feed the plant until the big leaves grow. Leaves have a special way of using air and sunlight to make plant food.

Growing beans

Put some wet kitchen roll in a jar with some water.

Put some beans next to the glass.

Put the jar in a warm, light place. The beans will swell up until they split and sprout roots and shoots.

Waterways

Plants suck up the water they need through their waterways. These are very thin tubes inside the stems.

Try this

You will need:
- a big jar
- some food dye
- some white flowers

In the soil

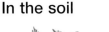

Worms pull leaves down into the soil.

Soil is full of things which are good for plants. Dead leaves, plants and tiny creatures rot away and make good plant food.

Put some water in the jar and add a few drops of food dye. Stand the flowers in it. After a few days the petal tips will change colour.

In two more days, the flowers will be the same colour as the dye. This is because the flowers suck the water and dye up into the petals.

Internet link Go to **www.usborne-quicklinks.com** and enter the keywords "pocket flower" for a link to a Web site where you can find out how to make a potato drink water.

Things you can grow

You can buy packets of flower and vegetable seeds in the shops. Here are some of the things you will need when you plant seeds for yourself.

– plant pots or yogurt pots
– a bag of compost
– a small watering can or jug
– a little trowel or an old spoon
– a plate
– some kitchen paper
– cress and sunflower seeds

Compost is a special soil with rich plant food in it.

Growing cress

Cress grows very easily and quickly at any time of the year.

Your cress will be ready to eat when it is about 7cm (3in) high.

You do not need soil, just some damp kitchen paper on a plate. Sprinkle some cress seeds on top.

Put the plate in a light place. The tiny shoots will soon grow, but you must keep the paper damp.

Sunflowers

In the spring you can start to grow sunflower seeds in pots.

Use a pot of compost for each seed. Push the seed in and sprinkle a little compost on top. Water the pots and put them in a warm, sunny place.

Try measuring the sunflowers to see how tall they grow.

After a few weeks shoots will appear and the plants will grow bigger. When they have four leaves they are big enough to plant in the garden.

Remember

Plants need these things to help them grow well.

They need sunlight to help them make their own special plant food.

They need water, but not too much, or they may rot.

They need soil because it gives them water and food.

Internet link Go to www.usborne-quicklinks.com and enter the keywords "pocket flower" for a link to a Web site where you can find some easy flowers to grow.

Where flowers grow

In the town

Gardens and parks are not the only places in towns where you might find flowers growing.

Some seeds are blown on to the roofs, where they grow.

Dandelion seeds get into the cracks in pavements.

The sowthistle grows in waste places and by the roadside.

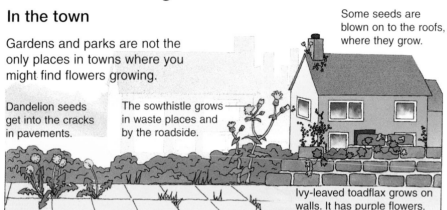

Ivy-leaved toadflax grows on walls. It has purple flowers.

In the country

Many wild flowers grow in different countries all over the world. These flowers grow in Europe.

The red horse chestnut tree has groups of flowers.

The sweet briar has pink flowers and prickly stems.

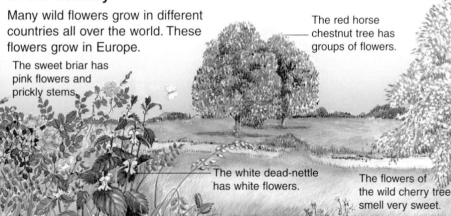

The white dead-nettle has white flowers.

The flowers of the wild cherry tree smell very sweet.

In hot places

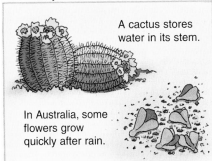

A cactus stores water in its stem.

In Australia, some flowers grow quickly after rain.

Desert plants have special ways of surviving without much rain.

In cold places

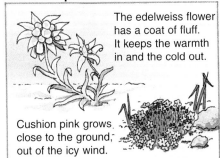

The edelweiss flower has a coat of fluff. It keeps the warmth in and the cold out.

Cushion pink grows close to the ground, out of the icy wind.

Plants which grow in cold, snowy places have ways of staying alive.

By the water

Some flowers grow well by the sea, by streams and other damp places.

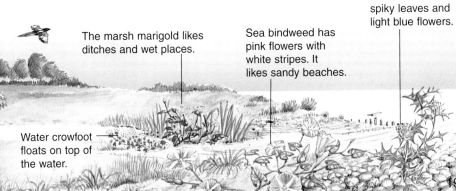

Sea holly grows on beaches. It has spiky leaves and light blue flowers.

The marsh marigold likes ditches and wet places.

Sea bindweed has pink flowers with white stripes. It likes sandy beaches.

Water crowfoot floats on top of the water.

19

Amazing plant facts

Many strange plants and flowers grow in parts of the world. They are all sorts of amazing shapes and sizes. Some even eat small animals.

The giant cactus

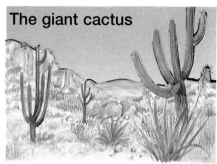

The saguaro is the largest cactus in the world. It grows as high as 15m (50ft) and lives for over 200 years.

The biggest flowers

The rafflesia flower is also very smelly.

The flower of the rafflesia plant is the biggest flower in the world. It measures nearly 1m (3ft) across.

Tiny plants

The smallest flowering plant is a kind of duckweed. It is so tiny that it looks like scum on the water.

Internet link *Go to* **www.usborne-quicklinks.com** *and enter the keywords "pocket flower" for a link to a Web site where you can find out more about the saguaro cactus.*

Flower traps

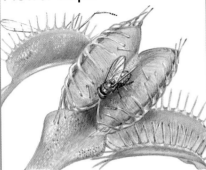

The Venus fly trap has spiky leaves. They snap shut to catch insects and tiny animals inside.

The sundew plant has leaves with sticky blobs. Insects stick to them and are eaten as plant food.

The oldest pot plant

A man grew a plant in a pot in Vienna in 1801. It is still alive today

The strongest water lily

The victoria amazonica water lily is strong enough for a child to stand on its thick, floating leaves.

Internet link Go to **www.usborne-quicklinks.com** and enter the keywords "pocket flower" for a link to a Web site where you can learn more about the Venus fly trap.

Useful words

You can find all of these words in this book.

hay fever
People with hay fever sneeze when there is a lot of pollen in the air.

insect
This is a small animal with 6 legs and a body made of 3 parts. A bee is an insect and so is a butterfly and an ant.

nectar
This is sweet liquid food inside a flower. Small visitors come to drink it. Bees use it to make honey.

pistil
New seeds grow in this part of the flower. It is also called the seed box.

pollen
This is the name for tiny golden specks on a flower. It makes new seeds grow in another flower.

roots
These parts of a plant grow down into the ground. They take in water and goodness from the soil.

sepals
These wrap around a bud to keep it safe while it is growing.

shoots
These are the new parts of a plant.

stamen
This part of a flower has pollen at the end.

stem
This is the stalk of a plant. It holds the flowers up, above the ground.

stigma
This flower part is sticky. Pollen from another flower sticks to it easily.

waterways
These are thin tubes inside a plant stem. The plant drinks water through them, to stay alive and to grow.

Internet links

Go to **www.usborne-quicklinks.com** and enter the keywords "pocket flower" for links to the following Web sites where you can find out more about flowers and plants and how they grow.

WEB SITE 1 See how to plan and grow a flower or vegetable garden.

WEB SITE 2 Find out why worms are good for gardens.

WEB SITE 3 Help Detective LePlant unravel the mystery of plant life.

WEB SITE 4 Watch a short movie on pollination, take a quiz or print out a diagram to colour.

WEB SITE 5 Take a virtual tour of an amazing children's garden and explore a maze, climb a tree house or find plants that dinosaurs ate.

WEB SITE 6 Find lots of ideas for fun garden projects at home, in the community or at school.

WEB SITE 7 Easy-to-follow tips for growing flowers, vegetables and herbs. Includes a helpful glossary.

WEB SITE 8 Find out how bees make honey, communicate by dancing and build their homes with wax.

WEB SITE 9 Fun experiments, information and a quiz explain all about different kinds of plants and flowers, and how they grow.

WEB SITE 10 Can you grow the ingredients you need to make a pizza? Play an online game to find out.

WEB SITE 11 Read about record breaking plants such as the oldest, tallest and most poisonous plants.

Internet safety: When using the Internet, please follow the safety guidelines shown on the Usborne Quicklinks Web site.

Index

First published in 2001 by Usborne Publishing Ltd., Usborne House, 83-85 Saffron Hill, London EC1N 8RT, England.